SUPER SCIENTISTS

HEAVENS ABOVE

KENNETH IRELAND

Illustrated by Peter Bull Art Studio

MACDONALD YOUNG BOOKS

Galileo cuts short his holiday

It was July 1609. Galileo Galilei, the famous inventor, was in Venice – on holiday. He'd only been there a day and already somebody was spoiling it for him.

"Tell me again," he said grimly.

His old friend Paolo Sarpi, who had a very important job with the government of Venice, was explaining the news.

"Hans Lippershey. He's a spectacle-maker from Holland," explained Paolo. "He's put a couple of spectacle lenses into a tube. And when you look through the tube, things that are miles away seem to be right in front of you."

Galileo wished he'd thought of the idea first. The Venetian government would pay a fortune for something like that. Their army and navy would fall over themselves to get their hands on it. And Galileo needed the money.

"Now look," he said sternly, "if this Lippershey turns up here, say you're too busy to see him. In the meantime I'll make one for you – I'll call it a telescope."

And cutting his holiday short, Galileo promptly dashed back home to Padua.

Working it out

The trouble was, Galileo
had very little idea of
how a telescope
might work. So he
picked up a piece
of lead tubing and
looked at it.

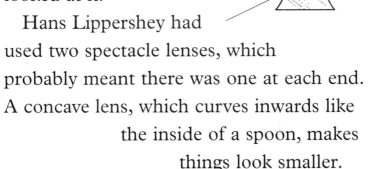

Hans Lippershey had
used two spectacle lenses, which
probably meant there was one at each end.
A concave lens, which curves inwards like
the inside of a spoon, makes
things look smaller.

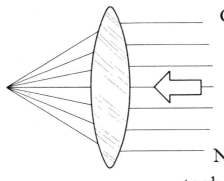

Galileo knew that.
A convex lens,
which curves
outwards, makes
things look bigger.
Now supposing he
took one of each...

He went to see a glassmaker.

"I want you to make lots of glass balls,"
he said, "then cut lenses of all different
thicknesses and shapes out of them."

As soon as the glassmaker had made them, Galileo started trying out all sorts of different concave and convex lenses, one at each end of a tube.

Before long, after many experiments, he found that two of the lenses made distant objects come three times closer. He changed the shape of them a little and tried again. And again.

Finally, "Got it!" he shouted. "Sixty times closer than they really are!"

Astonishingly it had taken him only twenty-four hours of trial and error to make his telescope. But he still needed to hurry. He had heard a rumour that Hans Lippershey was already on his way to Venice.

Galileo sent an urgent message to Paolo
Sarpi. "I have a secret," was all it said.

Sarpi knew exactly what he meant, and
the Dutchman never got past his door. And
it was no use trying to show his invention to
anyone else in Venice. After all,
Paolo Sarpi *was* the
scientific adviser to
the Venetian
government.

The Doge is very impressed

"Absolutely amazing," said the President of the Republic of Venice, known as the Doge.

It was two weeks later. The Doge, his advisers and the admirals of the Venetian navy were taking it in turns to peer through Galileo's already-improved telescope from the top of Saint Mark's Cathedral.

They had seen Padua, thirty-five miles away, really clearly. They could even make out Conegliano more than fifty miles away. Now one of the advisers turned his attention to the island of Murano.

"I can even see the people as they go into church!" he said excitedly.

"Never mind them," said one of the admirals, taking over the telescope and looking out to sea with it.

He stared for a moment in disbelief.

"There are some ships on the horizon. Without this telescope it would be another two hours before anyone would even know they were there."

That settled it. Every Venetian ship needed a telescope – and there were a great many ships in the Venetian navy.

Then the army thought they should have some telescopes as well...

Galileo's fortune was made. It was a pity about Hans Lippershey, of course. But then, he wasn't as smart as Galileo – nor did he have such an important friend as Paolo Sarpi.

The big surprise

A few months later, Galileo was back
home in Padua.

He had spent the afternoon looking after
his vines and flowers. But now it was evening.
There would be a new moon that night and
he wanted to watch it rise behind the domes
of the church at the end of the garden.

He took his telescope with him to a room
on the top floor which overlooked the
garden, then set it up at the window and
waited for the moon to appear. As soon as it
peeped from behind the domes of the
church he started looking at it.

At first he didn't believe his eyes.
Everyone thought that the moon was smooth
and polished, like a mirror. But through his
telescope it looked nothing like that.

In fact the moon looked more like dry,
dirty stone. He could even see mountains
rising out of it and large round craters all
over it.

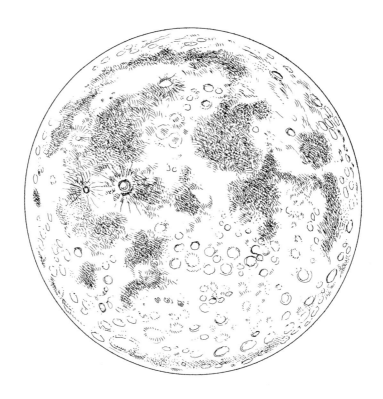

Galileo was so surprised that the next night he looked at it again, just to make sure. And for many nights after that, he drew sketches of the different things he kept seeing as the moon changed shape.

One morning, two months later,

"I still need to see things more clearly," he said, yawning. "I simply must have a more powerful telescope.

21

So he went to see the glassmaker again.
The next full moon was only a few days
away. He had to be ready by then. To save
time, he polished the glassmaker's lenses
himself. Soon he had made a telescope so
powerful it could magnify things an
astonishing four
hundred times.

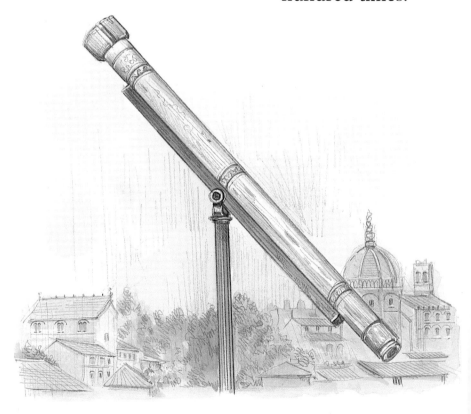

"I was right!" he said in triumph as he finally looked at the moon through it.

Now all he had to do was make more accurate sketches of what he had seen before.

And five successful telescopes later (he actually made a hundred, but wasn't really very good at grinding lenses and most of them didn't work) he suddenly found he had made one which could bring things a thousand times closer!

So he started looking at the stars and what we now know are planets. And that's when he got an even bigger surprise.

The Starry Messenger

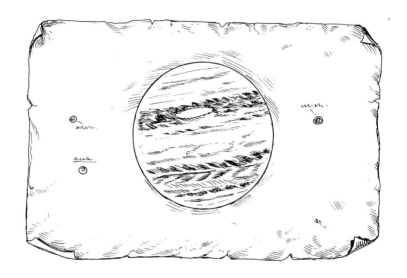

Galileo didn't know what to make of it.

On 7 January 1610, he had watched the planet Jupiter rise. Through his powerful new telescope he could see three small bright stars near it, two to the east and one to the west. He had drawn a little sketch of them and gone to bed.

But the next night two of the stars had moved! Now all three of them were on the west side of the planet.

A few nights later, one of them had disappeared completely. And a few nights after that, suddenly there were four of them.

This didn't make sense. Everyone knew that the sun, the planets and all the stars were fixed in the sky and moved only round the earth. The Bible said so. Besides, everyone could see that's what they did.

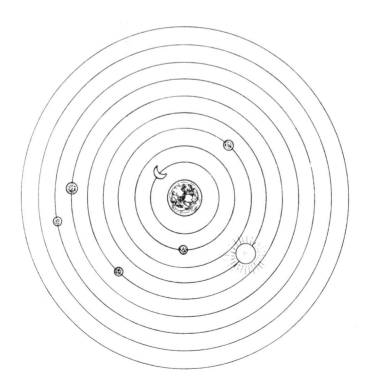

Galileo decided he'd
better find out what was going on.
So every night for the next six weeks he
watched Jupiter move across the sky, drew
sketches each time and tried to work out
where the stars would go next.

And at last he knew exactly what to make of it. He had solved one of the mysteries of the universe!

"Copernicus was right!" he shouted. They could hear him all over the house.

About seventy years before, Nicolaus Copernicus had said that all the stars and planets moved round the sun, instead of round the earth as everyone thought. But he'd never been able to prove it.

Neither had Galileo – not quite. But he could prove that stars could move round a planet which was itself moving. And that the moon moved round the earth – as the earth *itself* moved. The earth was not standing still while everything else in the sky moved round it after all.

It was an amazing discovery. And quite a shock. Galileo decided to write a book on everything he had discovered about the moon and the stars. He called it *The Starry Messenger*. It was one of the most important books of the seventeenth century.

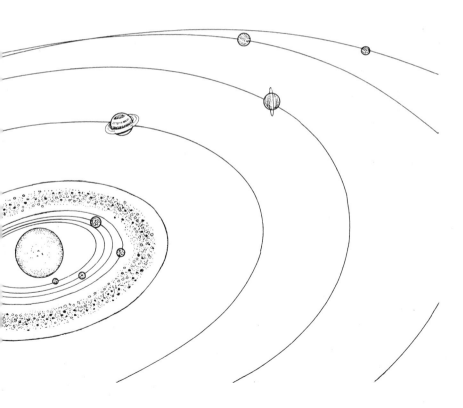

Excitement everywhere

Before long, people in every country in
Europe were reading *The Starry Messenger*.
And those who couldn't read were being
told about it by others who could.

Scientists said that Galileo's discoveries
were greater even than those of any of the
famous explorers – including Christopher
Columbus.

Poets even wrote poems about him.

Galileo, of course, was delighted. He was
even more delighted when suddenly
everyone who could afford one wanted to
buy a telescope.

Early one morning, one proud new owner carried his telescope to the bell tower of St Mark's Cathedral in Venice. An enormous crowd gathered, chased him up the stairs and kept him there for hours while they all had a look through the telescope.

The Queen of France was so excited when she first looked through hers that she fell to her knees in front of it – to the great surprise of the entire French court.

Her husband was very impressed. He wrote to Galileo. "In case you discover any other fine star, will you name it Henri, after me?" he asked.

Unfortunately King Henri of France was murdered a month later, so Galileo didn't use his name after all. But that gave Galileo an idea. He had called one of the new stars Cosimo, which was the name of the Duke of Tuscany. Now he sent the Duke his best telescope, with a letter.

In the letter he told the Duke how to find the star named after him. Then he added that the Duke might like to buy more telescopes for all his friends and most important allies.

Duke Cosimo was very grateful. So was Galileo very soon afterwards. The Duke not only bought lots of telescopes – he offered Galileo a job with a very high salary, as Chief Mathematician of Tuscany.

Galileo makes a mistake

"Glad to see your book's doing so well,"
said Galileo's old friend Paolo Sarpi.

"Have a copy for yourself," said Galileo,
giving him one. "But I've been doing other
things since then. I've been looking at
sunspots."

Galileo wasn't sure what they were. But for some time he had been watching black patches that kept appearing on the sun, especially at sunset. The only things certain about them was that they weren't stars or planets.

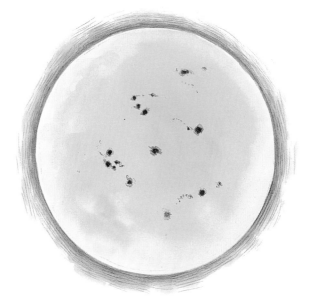

When he let Paolo look at sunspots through his telescope later that evening, Paolo didn't know what to make of them either. That was when Galileo told him that he was moving to Florence.

"I wouldn't if I were you," said Paolo anxiously. "What about the Pope?"

"What's the Pope got to do with it?" Galileo demanded.

"He's the head of the Christian Church. What if he decides that what you say about the stars is different from what it says in the Bible? He might want to punish you. Once you leave Venice we shan't be able to protect you."

Despite his friend's advice, Galileo decided to go anyway.
It was a big
mistake.

In May 1632 a cardinal, one of the most important men in the Church, went to see the Pope in Rome. "In the Bible it says that God makes everything in the heavens move round the earth," the cardinal said angrily. "But Galileo's just written yet another book. Now he says that he can *prove* the earth goes round the sun, not the other way round."

"I think we'd better send for Galileo," said the Pope grimly.

Prisoner!

At his trial Galileo was found guilty of heresy – meaning not agreeing with the teachings of the Church. He was sent to the palace of the Archbishop of Siena, where he was to be imprisoned until the Pope decided to let him go.

The happy times were now over. Galileo was seventy years old, and not very well. He might be a prisoner for the rest of his life.

However, the Archbishop gave him the best room in the palace, invited all Galileo's friends to visit him, and even sent for lenses so that Galileo could make another telescope.

The Pope was very annoyed when he heard how well Galileo was being treated. Galileo had asked many times to be moved to the village of Arcetri, to be near his favourite daughter who was in a convent there. So that was where the Pope now sent him. However, the local priests were to be in charge of him. They were told he had to live alone and never see more than one or two people at any time.

Galileo wrote one last book. But his sight was already failing, and for the last few years of his life he was completely blind.

He died in 1642.

Galileo was right!

On 31 October 1992, in the Vatican, the Pope and the Cardinals listened to what Cardinal Poupard had to tell them about Galileo.

He had only three things to say.

Firstly, hundreds of years ago, the writers of the Bible could only describe what they could see for themselves. So it wasn't surprising if they sometimes got it wrong. The stars, for instance.

Secondly, in Galileo's time, people believed the Bible's explanation of the stars. And they didn't like *anyone* telling them otherwise.

Finally, it was high time the Church admitted that Galileo had been right all along.

"I quite agree," said the Pope.

The next morning the news was on television and radio, and in newspapers all over the world: Galileo was right!

The Vatican has its own observatory now, with a huge telescope.

Galileo would have been pleased!

Timeline

Galileo Galilei was born on 15 February 1564, in Pisa, Italy.

1583	Invents the pendulum, supposedly after watching a lamp swinging in Pisa Cathedral.
1589	Legend says that he drops balls of different weights and sizes from the Leaning Tower of Pisa to prove that everything falls at the same speed.

1593	Invents the thermometer.
1596	Invents a gunsight to find the exact angle a gun needs to be set at to hit its target.
1597	Alters his gunsight so that it can be used for map-making and surveying – invents the theodolite.
1609	Makes his first telescope.
1610	*The Starry Messenger* is published.
1631	*A Dialogue Concerning the Two Chief World Systems* is published.
1633	Sentenced to prison for heresy.

Galileo Galilei died on 8 January 1642 at Arcetri, Italy. He was 77 years old.

Glossary

Astronomer	A scientist who studies space, the stars and planets
Dialogue	Two or more people talking
Lens	The curved glass used in things such as spectacles and telescopes
Magnify	To make things look bigger
Mathematician	Someone who studies mathematics
Scientific	To do with science
Sunspot	A dark patch on the sun's surface
Telescope	This word is made up of two Greek words: 'tele' means 'far off' and 'skopeð' means 'look at'
Universe	The sun, stars and planets
Venice	In Galileo's time, this was the capital city of one of the important countries in Europe, the Republic of Venice

---

WARNING
Never look at the sun through a
telescope or binoculars.
You could seriously damage your eyes.
